THE BULLY BRIGADE: THE TURNOVER

BY

T.T. FLOYD

Overflow Press

ISBN-13: 978-1-7329513-1-0

ACKNOWLEDGMENTS

I wish to express my sincere gratitude to my editor Jefferson for his guidance and critique of this manuscript.

I would also like to thank my cover design artist Lisa Beta for creating an awesome cover for this book.

Finally, I would like to thank my loving husband David, my mother and father Joseph and Barbara Wiggins, and my spiritual mother and father Ron and Stephanie Harper. Thank you for your love, dedication, support, and always believing in me. You are appreciated!

To Mrs.Willie Mae McClain, David, Jr., Taylor, and Dylan

Chapter 1

It was a sunny morning at Misfit Elementary School. Students were running rampant on the hardcourt, laughing hysterically. Some were chasing others with booey-gooey boogers, some were taunting kids, playing monkey in the middle with the others' belongings, and some were jumping rope and playing basketball and hopscotch. Then there was the Brigade: Petey, Diego, Ruthie, Pudge, Bustah, and Charlie. They were hovering over a terrified boy lying bound on the ground. He was screaming bloody murder, but his cries were muffled by a lime-green bandana handkerchief stuffed in his mouth, and he was bound by a rugged tan jump rope. As he tried anxiously to wiggle himself out of the terrifying contraption, Charlie, a girl with orange curly hair, straddled him.

"You're mine now, pooty breath!" she said as she sank her right knee into his chest. "You betta not eva take his lunch money again, you hear me? Or else. His mama worked hard, and I mean hard, for that money!"

"Yeah, hard!" the rest of the gang said in unison.

"Ya not tryin' to make him starve, are ya? Are ya?!"

"No!" squealed the little boy. Beads of sweat rolled down his cherry-pie-red face. His head moved up and down rapidly.

"I don't think ya understand. Does he look like he could miss a meal? Huh?! But you sure can, tubby tubby! Pass me the newspaper, Ruthie."

Ruthie handed her the newspaper, and she balled it up and WHACK! Right upside his head, it

2

went. "Maybe that'll knock some sense into ya. Now, get missin'!"

"What's the damage?" said the scrawny victim as a sigh of relief highlighted his face.

"Well," said Charlie, "there's two, four, six of us at twenty-five cents apiece. That'll be a dollar fifty."

"Cool," said the boy. "Here ya go!"

"Thanks!"

The late bell rang, and the crew huddled together. "Bully who?!" yelled Bustah.

"Respect the crew!" shouted the crew.

"See you guys at lunch," said Charlie.

Charlie was a fighter. In a good way. She hated to see her peers mistreated. She was bold, loud, and strong. That was actually how she and Ruthie had become good friends. One day in second grade, everyone was sitting on the bleachers watching the fourth and fifth graders battle each other in a game of softball. It was the third inning. Charlie kept seeing this twinkling light that caused her to squint really bad. "What is that?!" she said. She heard a giggle and turned to Ruthie, who was too into the ballgame to even notice.

"Go fourth graders!" yelled Ruthie. Suddenly, she looked down and saw a corner of her reflection staring back at her and the pink and purple flowered panties under Ruthie's dress. Her eyes elevated back up in horror and became fixated on the two boys.

"Ruthie, watch out!"

Charlie plunged across Ruthie and grabbed the little boy by the neck. Back and forth they rocked as one of the boys tried with all his might to pull away. The other boy was able to escape immediately.

"You ol' dirty dog! Ladies are to be respected!" she yelled, as the little boy eagerly squirmed away. "How would you like it if I did that to ya mama? You wouldn't laugh then!"

The boy and Charlie scuffled across Ruthie, and his foot knocked the mirror to the ground. As the mirror fell, Ruthie took one look at it and screamed, "Ahhh! Ahhh!" She then joined forces with Charlie and began giving the boy wet willies and twisting his nose.

A few minutes later, Ruthie and Charlie's dilemma became the main event, flooded with spectators. Mrs. Belcherton, the counselor, came running over to the bleachers. Charlie had the boy locked in a full nelson. He looked disturbingly embarrassed.

"Charlie Copay and Ruthendra Revere stop this foolishness right now!" said Mrs. Belcherton.

"What foolishness?" said Charlie as she continued to hold the boy in a full nelson. "You must mean justice, because that's what we were seekin'. These two toilet lickers were using a mirror to look under Ruthie's dress!"

"We were not!" yelled the boy.

"Release him, Charlie! Is this true, boys?" asked Mrs. Belcherton.

Charlie released the poor boy from the wrestling hold, and he said in a sad voice, "No. We were doing an experiment on birds. We...we...we thought that if the light reflected on their faces, we would be able to capture them."

"Baloney!!!" yelled Ruthie. "You can't see a bird in a mirror if it's under my dress."

"You boys are in big trouble," said Ms. Belcherton. "Do you know that this could be held against you in a court of law? You must think before you act. I'm calling all four of your parents and informing them of this fiasco. I will see you guys in my office at 9 a.m. tomorrow for mediation. Exit the field and go home now!"

The girls headed across the field, kicking up orange dust as they dragged their feet in the dirt.

"I want another go at those idiots. They should be under the jail," said Charlie.

"Yeah, under the jail and in the sewer with the rats!" exclaimed Ruthie. They chuckled. Ruthie wrapped her arm around Charlie's neck. "Thanks for having my back, Charlie. It really means a lot."

"No problem. Us girls have got to stick together."

The two had been inseparable ever since.

Chapter 2

"Rrrrrriiiiiinnnnng! Rrrrrriiiiiinnnnnnng!" The late bell rang, and the gang rushed to their lines for class pick-up. Charlie, Diego, and Bustah were in Mr. Funkberry's class, while Ruthie, Petey, and Pudge were in Mrs. Goozerbee's class. Both classes were across the hall from one another. The students filed into Mr. Funkberry's class one by one.

"Good morning, kiddo diddos. Today, let's see which way the wind blows," said Mr. Funkberry as he pulled up the radar map of the weather forecast for the day on the tech board. The students watched in amazement as the rain and wind gusts on the radar danced to the east. "Hmmm. Are we safe from the storms today, Bustah?"

"No, Mr. Funkberry," replied Bustah, "because Krystal is mad that I dumped her yesterday. I gave her my last powdered donut, and she gave it to

Xavier. And she know how I feel about my powdered donuts!" He licked his lips, rubbed his stomach, and stomped his foot two times. "If only I could still taste it," he added as he gave Krystal a fierce glance across the room. "So, I expect the forecast to be cloudy with heavy thunderstorms because she'll probably be crying, 'My baby dumped me!' all day."

The whole class laughed. Krystal snarled and rolled her eyes at Bustah.

"Why, thank you, Bustah," Mr. Funkberry said, "for your traditional morning humor boomer, but the real answer is that since the storm appears to be moving east and we live in the west, we are safe, and there will be no thunderstorms!"

Mr. Funkberry was a cool dude. He was tall as a light pole, dark-skinned, and slim, with a humungous afro and a well-groomed goatee. He always wore flip-flops, and he always spoke in a poetic tone. He was so cool that he had been voted best teacher three years in a row. Another reason why he was so cool was because he kept a sweet stash of snacks and goodies for the students who always came to school with empty bellies. Occasionally, he would play the drums for the whole class if they did all their work. Sometimes, the student who participated the most would get a chance to be a Funkaroo for the day. The Funkaroo had the privilege of beating the drums while creating a wacky song with Mr. Funkberry. Most of the time, Bustah was the Funkaroo. Boy, did Bustah love music!

"Alright, class, said Mr. Funkberry, "go ahead and take out your math books while I take attendance. Peterson... Aristide..."

After three hours of learning how to tell time, author's point of view, and about force, motion, and energy, it was finally time for lunch.

"Alright, Funkaroos!" announced Mr. Funkberry. "Clear your desk, and let's see who's going to be Captain Funkaroo today."

Everyone wanted to be Captain Funkaroo. With intense urgency, the sounds of papers crumpling and books slamming echoed through the room as students scurried to tidy up their areas. One minute later, you could hear a pin drop, and everyone's hands were folded.

"Hmmm. I see that you guys are going to make this hard for me, huh? Oooookay! Who can tell me what time it will be in fifteen minutes?"

Half of the students eagerly raised their hand. "Oooh, ooh, I want to do it. Pick me! Pick me!" yelled the students.

"Diego. Tell me, what time will it be in fifteen minutes?" asked Mr. Funkberry.

Diego glanced at the clock. "Currently, it is 10:43 a.m. In fifteen minutes, it will be 10:58 a.m.," he proudly stated.

"My man!" exclaimed Mr. Funkberry. Diego and Mr. Funkberry slapped fives. "Let's skedaddle, Funkaroo!" said Mr. Funkberry.

All the students lined up quietly behind Diego. His eyes lit up with excitement.

"March and repeat after me, amigos!" he said. "Andale! Andale! Let's get ready for lunch today!"

The other students clapped their hands to the beat and chimed in merrily. As they marched out of the room, Petey and Ruthie looked on.

"Oh, how I wish that we were in Mr. Funkberry's class. It's such a kid-friendly class," said Petey.

"I know, right?!" said Ruthie.

"Straighten up my line now!" yelled Mrs. Goozerbee.

"I swear she was a drill sergeant in her former life," murmured Petey.

"You are to walk quietly to the cafeteria," said Mrs. Goozerbee. "If I hear one peep out of you, you're going to lose twenty misfit bucks. Are we clear?"

"Yes, Mrs. Goozerbee!" said the class. Ruthie, Petey, Pudge, and the rest of the students rolled their eyes and walked quickly to the lunchroom.

In the lunchroom, students were sitting at the tables, playing board games, swapping snacks, and eating, while Mr. Funkberry's and Mrs. Goozerbee's classes stood in line to receive their lunches.

"Yaaay! We're having tacos!" said Petey.

"Tacos or tuna?" asked the server.

"Tacos," said Petey and Ruthie in unison.

The server placed two tacos, one scoop of corn, and a freeze pop on each of their plates. The clerk cashed them out, and then they walked quickly to their seats to chew and chat with the rest of the gang. Since all students had to sit with their classes, the gang sat back to back at the mobile stool tables. This way, while they were eating, they could turn around and talk to one another. Petey chomped away at his taco and turned toward Bustah.

"Yo, Bus, did you see the Sundevils game last night?" he asked with excitement.

"Yeah, man! They clobbered the JayCubs!" said Bustah.

"My dad was sooo mad he burned himself with his own cigarette!"

"What?! Wait a minute?" Bustah chuckled. "You must give me an instant replay of how that went down."

"Remember, right before halftime, when the JayCubs were up by two and Trivochec hit a three from half-court to tie the game?"

"Yeah."

"My dad jumped up and down and started pacing back and forth, puffing on his cigarette like this. Then, after half-time, when Mason and Ratfurt made a three again, he started wailing and slumped down and put his head between his legs and burned his thigh. He jumped up so fast, like a jack-in-the-box, and made this horse sound like this: Waaahahahah! It was too funny."

"That's funny. Do it again." Bustah was laughing so hard that he caught a cramp in his side.

As Petey jumped up, mimicking his father one last time, a yellow shell collided with the top of his head, and taco meat and sour cream rained down his face. Bustah's smile quickly turned to a frown. Bustah and Petey gave each other a deep, piercing stare.

"Who did this?" screamed Petey.

The gang slowly turned and looked at the beefy goo that covered Petey's face. They all stood up and looked around as the rest of the students giggled hysterically or stared in shock. Suddenly, an open carton of chocolate milk somersaulted through the air and soaked Penny Proudfoot's hair.

"Aaaaaaaaaaaaahhhhhhhhh!" she screamed. Everyone in the lunchroom chuckled except the gang. Penny stood up in rage. "Oh, you think this is funny, do you? Well, let's even the score," she snarled.

She picked up her open milk carton and threw it across the room at another table. She then continued to pick up item after item off her tray and fling it across the room rapid-fire. Quickly, pandemonium and chaos erupted as taco meat, shells, tuna, and milk started flying from the north, south, east, and west.

"Run for cover!" yelled Pudge.

He immediately rushed to the exit, only to be taken down by the smooth sour cream on the floor. When he slid on it, he flew backward, and his backside gave a hard kiss to the stiff tile. Petey, Ruthie, Bustah, and Diego immediately grabbed Pudge's legs and dragged him out of the cafeteria as they rushed to the exit.

"Goodness, are you okay?" asked Petey.

Pudge's face was beaming with embarrassment. He was so busy gasping for air that he could hardly speak.

"Yeah...I just need a minute," he finally said.

"This is loco," said Diego.

"In all of our years at Misfit Elementary, we've never had a food fight," said Ruthie.

A few minutes later, Charlie came running up behind them.

"Hey, Pudge are you okay?" she asked.

"Yeah, man, I just need a moment."

"I want to know which fool hit me in the head with a taco," said Petey.

"Yeah, me too," said Bustah. "It was total chaos, but you have to admit that it was amazing watching Penny Proudfoot get soaked in chocolate milk."

"Oh yeah," said Ruthie and Charlie in unison.

Penny Proudfoot was a snooty third grader who thought she owned the universe and everything in it. She often wore her hair in a bun and dressed in striped polo shirts, cardigans, shorts, and tennis skirts. Everything was a competition to Penny, from who answered the most questions right in class to who performed better at P.E. and who danced and sang the best. One time, she even tried to compete with Charlie over who could belch the loudest. She was competitively obnoxious.

After giving Diego a short time to recuperate, Diego and Bustah helped him to his feet.

"You might need to see the school nurse, Pudge," said Ruthie.

"I think you might be right," said Pudge while limping and holding the small of his back with his right hand.

"I'll walk you to the office." Ruthie gently wrapped her arms around Pudge's neck, and they walked off.

Just after they left, Principal Strongarm came rushing into the cafeteria with her crimson and cream-colored bullhorn. The gang looked at each other in suspense, and one by one, they walked back into the lunchroom.

Everyone involved in the chaos stopped dead in their tracks once they heard the principal's deep baritone voice say, "Shut it down right now! Have a seat! Security! Guard the doors and don't let anyone out! I'm going to ask this question one time. Who's responsible for all this chaos?"

Principal Strongarm was about four feet tall and a hundred pounds. She wore thick bifocal glasses. She was very strict and intimidating for her teeny-weeny stature.

No one responded. Instead, everyone looked at one another with suspicion. It was so quiet that for the first time, everyone could hear the air-conditioning unit.

"Since we have no clue who started this fiasco," said Principal Strongarm, "and food just seems to fly across the room on its own, I think we'll have silent lunch until the cowardly culprit comes forth."

As she made her way to the exit, she stopped and slowly pivoted back to the audience. "By the way, all extracurricular activities are canceled immediately. So, you want to act like animals that belong in a zoo? Oh, I'll show you that one monkey won't start a show."

Once Principal Strongarm had made her exit, heavy groans, murmurs, and sighs filled the room, and it became suffocated with resentment.

When the lunch period was over, the students filed out of the cafeteria class by class as the security guard called their teachers' names. The gang was very upset, and they exited the cafeteria with great disappointment. Mrs. Goozerbee was so upset about the incident that she made the entire class copy the first five pages of the dictionary. Mr. Funkberry decided that no one would be a Funkaroo for two weeks.

A few hours later, Mr. Funkberry's and Mrs. Goozerbee's classes went to P.E. As the other kids jumped rope and played basketball and kickball, the gang sat under the oak tree.

"Yo, what happened in the cafeteria was an absolute mess," said Bustah.

"I wonder which hammerknocka' did it," said Charlie.

"Yeah, because of them, I probably have arthritis in my hands from Mrs. Goozerbee making us copy the words out of the dictionary," said Ruthie.

"Mami, I feel your pain. Mr. Funkberry won't let us be Funkaroos for two weeks," said Diego.

"Well, hopefully by tomorrow, they'll find out who it is, and things can go back to normal," said Petey as he tossed the ball up in the air.

"Don't forget, you guys. We need to check up on Pudge after school," said Bustah.

"Of course!" said Ruthie.

"Now, let's not stand around and mope," said Petey. "Everything will be resolved by tomorrow. Dodgeball, let's play!"

The gang got into position and played a tough game of dodgeball. Of course, Bustah won since he was the most athletic and competitive.

After P.E., the students went back to their classes to prepare for dismissal. As the teachers distributed homework assignments, Mrs. Strongarm began the afternoon announcements.

"Good afternoon! Students, we must conduct ourselves in an orderly fashion at all times. I was appalled by your behavior at lunch earlier this afternoon and expect to see progress ASAP. That is not how students at Misfit Elementary behave. Whoever started that monstrosity, you will be caught. When I catch you, you will be fried!"

The dismissal bell rang, and the gang met up with each other in the hallway.

"Did you hear Mrs. Strongarm? Whoever did that mess is going to be fried," said Petey.

"I'm absolutely sure this will be resolved tomorrow," said Ruthie.

"We shall see," said Bustah.

As the gang prepared to cross the street and head to Pudge's house, the sound of an infamous voice stopped them in their tracks.

"Well, looky looky, it's the brown-nosin' ratcheteers trying to save the day," said a freckle-faced, honey-blond-haired boy.

"Uh, I can't stand this jerk," mumbled Charlie as they turned to face him.

It was the worst disaster ever: Andy Pitts and his sidekick, Pooch.

"Shut your dumpster, Andy Pitiful," said Bustah.

"Make me, Bustah," said Pitts. "What are you gonna do? Bust me up or watch me bust you in your head?"

Bustah dropped his bookbag on the sidewalk. "Pitts, I don't think you want this. But I can give it to you however you'd like. I can slice you, dice you, throw you, or stump you. Your pick."

Pitts walked closer to Bustah. "You won't do crap. You're just a little third-grade punk," he said as he pushed his finger into Bustah's chest.

Bustah quickly reacted with a left hook to Pitts's face.

Petey, Diego, and Pooch rushed in to break it up. "Romperlo! Romperlo!" yelled Diego.

"Oh, it's going down," said Pitts as Petey held him back.

"You think you're so hard, machismo?" said Diego.

"I don't care what grade you're in. I'll still dishrag you," said Bustah.

"Oh yeah, we'll see about that," said Pitts.

"Let's go, man," said Pooch as he pulled Pitts back. "Principal Strongarm is watching."

Diego and Pitts stared intensely at each other, and then Pitts and Pooch slowly walked away.

"Andy is just what his last name says...the pits," said Ruthie and Charlie in unison.

The gang walked two more blocks, singing their anthem as they marched: "Bully who? Respect the crew! Bully who? Respect the crew! Bully who? Respect the crew!."

The march came to a halt when they got to Pudge's house.

Chapter 3

"Mrs. Ruiz, it's Petey and the crew. Is anybody home?!"

Suddenly, the door clicked and swung open to reveal a tall, curly-haired brunette. "Hey, you guys!" she said with a saucy Latin accent as she greeted them with hugs. "How was school?"

"No bueno," said Diego.

"Yeah," said Bustah. "We came to check on Pudge after his tough fall today."

"How sweet. He'll be glad to see you! Come on in!"

The gang entered Pudge's powder blue bedroom, which had pictures of his favorite athletes and music artists plastered all over the walls and two model airplanes hanging from the ceiling. He was lying in the bed with his arms behind his head, staring at the ceiling.

"What's happening P?" Bustah asked.

"It's way too quiet in here," said Ruthie as she marched across the threshold. She grabbed the black remote and cut on the TV.

Then came Charlie, eager to help her injured friend. "Diego and I are going to make your favorite snack. Come on, Diego."

Petey and Bustah plopped down on the yellow bean bags. All Pudge could do was blush at the attention he was getting from the group. He loved the gang, and they loved him.

Bustah grabbed the remote from Ruthie and began flipping from channel to channel. "Isn't *Go-Go Rangers* on?" he asked.

"I think so," said Pudge. "Try Channel 23."

Diego and Charlie marched into the room with two trays. "One peanut butta and banana sandwich, a tall glass of homogenized milk, a fruit snack, and service with a smile," said Charlie as she graciously smiled at Pudge.

"Yo, amigos I got some honey buns, chicharrones, tortilla chips, salsa, and popcorn," said Diego.

Each of them snatched a snack off the tray.

"Oh yeah!" said Petey.

"Oh yeah yeah!" said Ruthie. "

"Oh yeah yippy yeah yeah!" said Bustah and Pudge in unison.

The gang laughed. They snacked, watched TV, played Pudge's favorite video game, Super Troopers 2, and listened to music. Close to 6 p.m., when everyone would have to head home, Bustah looked at Ruthie.

"Hey, Ruthie, do we have any clients on the list for tomorrow?"

"Clients...? Hmmm, let's see."

She reached into her neon pink and green book bag and grabbed a small red notebook with a hologram of six fists surrounding a peace sign.

"Oh yeah. We have Little Milton," she replied. "He is being harassed by Andy Pitts. According to my notes, Andy is forcing him to do things like stealing copy paper from the principal's office, and he's making Milton complete his homework. Poor Milton. So, who's going to take the lead on this job?"

"You know I will," said Bustah.

"Ok, then who's going to assist you?" asked Ruthie.

"I will!" yelled Charlie.

"Okeedokee," said Ruthie.

The gang continued to watch TV, laugh, and joke. Not long after, Pudge's mom stuck her head in the room. "Guys, It's 6 p.m."

"What ?!!" said Petey. Immediately, the gang sprouted up from their comfortable seats and scurried around the room, looking for their shoes and bookbags.

"Gotta go, Pudge!" they all said in unison.

"See ya in a few days," said Charlie.

"Feel better," said Ruthie.

"Take it easy, homes," said Diego.

"Hang tough, man!" said Petey.

Chapter 4

The next morning, the gang waited patiently under the tree for Ruthie so that they could start their meeting.

"Hey guys, sorry I'm late. My mom burned a hole in my favorite shirt, so I had to find my second favorite shirt."

The gang sighed.

"Not your Nacho Taco shirt with the Mexican gray wolf on the front," said Petey.

"Yep…that's the one," she replied.

"We're so sorry to hear that, Ruthie," said Charlie.

"Yeah, I'm still in mourning. Anyways, back to business. So, Charlie and Bustah are taking care of

Pitts for bullying Milton. So, what does this plan look like?"

"We can't come at him directly like we would with the other bullies," said Charlie.

"Why not?" asked Bustah.

"Because it's too predictable."

"Well, Andy is on the school basketball team, so let's just ambush him in the locker room," Petey suggested.

"Really? I know we have better ideas than that!" said Diego.

"How about we deflate the basketballs before the next game and lock his sidekick in the boiler room?" suggested Bustah.

"Now, that's a slappin', spankin' idea," said Charlie, "but with Pitts being a little older than us, he's probably not intimidated by us."

"Then what do you suggest we do?" asked Ruthie.

"Let's put a little laxative in his food so that he's freaked out," said Pudge.

"Uh, no. He could be allergic to the laxative. Come on, you guys! We're not trying to go to jail. We're just trying to create peace in a non-violent way!"

"What do you mean non-violent?" asked Diego. "Charlie just tied a cucaracha down with a rope for some lunch money."

Ruthie shrugged. "We're kids. Growth is a process. Duh! We'll get there."

"How much is this job?" asked Bustah.

"A dollar fifty," said Ruthie.

"We need to increase the price," said Charlie. "This is Pitts we're dealin' wit', which means that we're gonna have to provide a high quality of service. So, we may want to up the price to three dollars."

"Can't argue with that!" said Petey.

Ruthie, Bustah, and Charlie slapped fives.

"I got it!" Petey yelled excitedly. "Let's beat him at his own game...literally."

"No way. You mean play basketball?" asked Ruthie.

"Yep."

"What do you mean no way?" asked Bustah.

"Yeah, and I'm a great rebounder," said Petey.

"Yeah, and I'm awesome at getting fouled!" exclaimed Diego with an evil grin. The gang giggled hysterically.

"I make a great coach," said Charlie.

"And I make the best healthy snacks and lunches," said Ruthie.

"So, I guess this means it'll be three on three," said Bustah.

"Does everyone agree?" asked Charlie.

"Yep, three on three, it is," they all said.

Three hours later, it was time for lunch. What the students of Misfit elementary had once longed for, they had now begun to dread. Lunchtime. The students trudged reluctantly to the cafeteria and moped as they received their lunches and sat down. You could have heard a pin drop. These silent lunches were beginning to take a toll on them.

"Be forewarned," Bustah said to Ruthie. "This may be the only action we get today." He leaned his head in Pitts's direction.

"Nooo," whispered Ruthie as her eyes stretched wide. "Don't do it. Not now." She pitter-pattered her feet against Bustah's leg. *We'll have longer lunches,* she mimed as she stretched her two index fingers apart and rubbed her right palm on her stomach in a circular motion.

Being the brash kid he was, Bustah took matters into his own hands anyway.

"Yo, Pitts, I hear you like making punk moves like bullying other people to do things, and that's a problem," he said as he stared at Pitts.

"It's little punks like you that jump up to get beat down. So, if you wanna break glass, we can get it crackin' pronto," replied Pitts as his fist and palm collided.

Bustah walked over to Pitts, looked him square in the eye, and said, "Put your best squad together and meet me on the court two Fridays from now at five o'clock sharp. The first team that wins two out of three games wins. If your squad wins, we'll do your homework for a week. If our squad wins, then you have to leave our client alone and help us restore order in the cafeteria."

"Uh, not so fast. When I mop the floor with you dweebs, you and your minions will do my homework for a month and mow my lawn. Either way this goes, you're gonna owe me."

"We won't owe you nothin'."

"We'll see about that."

Bustah bumped shoulders with Pitts as they walked past each other and then off in opposite directions. The gang walked away cool, calm, and collected.

"Charlie, meet me at my house after school," said Ruthie. "As for the rest of you, our first practice will be on Friday at Knuckles Flat."

"Knuckles Flat?" asked Bustah. "It's always crowded there. Plus, the beasts who play there are ruthless. Players always fight on that court."

"That's the whole point. We're meeting there to play them. They'll help prepare us for battle. Bring a change of clothes. We'll go straight after school."

"Alright, I guess," said Bustah.

"The sound of reluctance in your voice is not very becoming of you, Bus," said Charlie.

As soon as the school bell rang, Charlie raced out of class to meet up with Ruthie, who was standing ahead of her, and she locked her right arm around Ruthie's left arm.

"Let's go," said Ruthie. "We have work to do. My house or your house?"

"Your house!" Charlie said as she gave one strong nod.

"Indeed, it is."

The girls finally reached Ruthie's house.

"Ok. First things first," said Charlie as she took out her notebook. "We need to make an agenda. Here we go."

Charlie paced up and down the room like a madwoman. The click-clack of her ragged leather boots on the creaky-squeaky hardwood floors usually would have been nerve-wracking to Ruthie, but

Ruthie's excitement about the plan overshadowed that emotion.

"Ok," said Charlie, "write this down. Things to do by Friday." As she spoke, she marched in place. She always did when she became excited about something, and that was when her best ideas came to her.

"First, we need to research basketball drills and come up with a pre- and post-basketball workout. Second...we need an extra basketball with us at all times in case something happens to the main one. Third...we must videotape the team's practice on Thursday so that we can identify our strengths and weaknesses. Fourth...we must have chewing gum. Research shows that chewing gum helps you concentrate."

"Fifth..." Ruthie interjected.

"We must practice with the guys in the event one of them gets hurt, and sixth...we have to assign them to a practice team. Oh, and by the way, we have to go video Andy and the team practicing before our first practice. Done!"

"Ok. Let's research some pre- and post-basketball workouts," said Ruthie as she opened the laptop.

That night, Ruthie and Charlie worked diligently on a pre-and post-basketball workout plan. They coordinated basketball drills, researched the different positions, and determined which person would play which position based on speed and physical strength. They even created and printed a list of healthy snacks packed with a nice balance of proteins, fats, and carbs for the team.

"OMG! It's nine o'clock," said Charlie. "I have to get home. Good job, partner. We've covered a lot of ground."

"Yes, we did," replied Ruthie. "Ok. So, now that this is complete, let's see what's next on our agenda."

"We have to videotape them practicin' tomorrow. So, we'll tell them their positions and see what they're workin' wit'. Gimme a high five, girl. We're on a roll!"

Chapter 5

The next morning, the light of the sun gazed at Charlie through her bedroom window, waking her up.

"It's practice day, it's practice day!" she yelled as she pumped her fist in the air. She smiled back at the sun, stretched her toes and arms, and literally rolled out of bed and onto the floor with a loud bump.

"Charlie!" her mother called.

"I'm okay!" Charlie yelled back.

She rolled back and forth on the floor with excitement for a good minute. She then got up, got dressed, grabbed her basketball, and left for school.

The gang met up under the oak tree near the hardcourt, like they did every morning before school. They were chatting it up about which video games on the market were the best when, out of nowhere, Charlie interrupted.

"Hey, you guys! I'm so excited about practice today," she sang as she ruffled the orange curls in her hair with her hands, rapidly jogging in place and turning around in circles at the same time. The gang chuckled, as did the children around them.

"You're such a nut, Charlie Copay!" exclaimed Ruthie.

"I know, right? I just can't wait for practice today."

"It's going to be awesoooome!" they both yelled.

Suddenly, the bell rang.

"See you guys after school," said Charlie.

Once school was out, the gang rushed to Knuckles Flat for a spot on the court. Ruthie and Charlie asked some of the guys on the court if they would play a game with them and give them some pointers, but they were so focused on winning their own high-stakes games that they declined.

"Okay, guys," said Ruthie. "Welcome to basketball camp. Our first game is in two weeks, so the first thing I want to do is start with a pre-basketball workout. Okay, everybody spread out. Give each other space using arm's distance."

Charlie extended both of her arms out to display arm's distance for the team.

"Okay, so Charlie is going to demonstrate the first exercise for you, which is skipping."

Charlie's long legs skipped up and down the court as her orange ponytail swayed left and right, left and right.

"Now you guys try it," said Ruthie. "Remember, it's not a race, so go at your own pace."

"This workout is going to be a piece of a cake," said Bustah.

Charlie put both of her index fingers up and moved them up and down near her freckled cheeks as she sarcastically stated in a squeaky voice, "Oh, we shall see!"

"Next exercise, jumping jacks. Give me fifty," said Ruthie.

Once the gang had done fifty jumping jacks, Petey yelled, "No sweat off my back! What's next?"

"Cocky, aren't we?" said Charlie.

"Don't insult the program, Petey. Like Nike, just do it!" said Ruthie.

The girls had strategically designed the workout so that the easy exercises would be done first, before the tough ones. Once the tough exercises were underway, those once happy-go-lucky high-cheeked smiles declined to low stankin' grins. The girls took turns demonstrating the harder exercises. Once the gang got through the butt kicks and backward running, it was the final exercise in the workout that was the real butt-kicker…alternating toe-to-hand kicks.

Charlie demonstrated by kicking up her right leg and touching her right toe with her left hand. Then she did the same with her left toe and right hand, changing hands and legs as she made her way across the basketball court.

"What!" yelled Pudge. "My legs are too fat and short for that."

"Oh, stop making excuses, Pudge," said Ruthie. "Let's go! Get that leg up there."

The gang was struggling badly.

"You guys have no coordination whatsoever!" yelled Charlie. "Ya look like a broke-down group of raggedy ostriches. Let's go! When ya kick, those legs should be straight."

Everyone had finished their last kick, and they were all lying sprawled on the concrete except for Pudge. He had struggled through the last few kicks and was getting ready for his final kick. As sweat dripped from his face, and with his hands on his knees and his chest inhaling and exhaling rapidly, he whined, "I can't do it!"

"Yes, you can. You got one more," said Charlie.

"You can do it!" cheered Ruthie.

Diego and Bustah walked over and grabbed Pudge's leg. "Andale, Andale! Lo tienes, dude. Lo tienes," said Diego.

Pudge allowed the guys to help him get through the last kick. As they picked his leg up, he wobbled a bit, and Petey grabbed his left hand and touched it to his right toe.

"Yayeee! We did it!" the gang shouted.

Pudge sprawled on the grass.

"Nice work, Pudge!" said the gang in unison.

"Wheeew! Now that we've got that out of the way, listen up for your positions," said Ruthie.

"Petey, you're playing center," said Charlie. "That means that it's a must that you get those rebounds. Pudge, you're a power forward. Diego, you're a small forward. Bustah, you're a point guard, and Milton will be the shooting guard. Today, we're playing three on three. Diego, Bustah, and Pudge, you're on a team. Petey, Milton, and Charlie, you're on the other team. This will be a thirty-minute game, so I'm setting my timer. After that, we'll do our post-workout. I'm going to videotape the game so that we all can see our weaknesses. Got it?"

"Got it!" said both teams.

"Alright! Positions, please," said Ruthie.

She dribbled the ball to the center circle of the court, and the gang huddled around her. She bounced the ball three times and tossed it in the air as high as she could.

Pudge jumped up and whacked the ball toward his side of the court, giving his team an opening advantage. He chased the ball down and then dribbled downcourt with it. He took a shot, but the ball bounced off the backboard. Luckily, he recovered the ball quickly and pushed it in the basket.

Petey grabbed the ball and took it down the court. He quickly passed it to Milton, who ran with it cradled in his arms to the basket and released it.

"Come on, Milton!" said Charlie. "You're traveling."

The ball hit the rim and bounced to the ground. Pudge swiftly grabbed it, raced downcourt, and leaped up for a successful jump shot.

"Good job, Pudge!" said Ruthie.

Now Charlie had the ball, and Bustah was guarding her. She dribbled and shuffled left, and then she dribbled and shuffled right for about a good five minutes.

"Milton, where are you?" she yelled.

"Over here," said Milton as he waved his arms.

She passed the ball to him, and once again, he cradled it in his hand and ran to the basket. This time, the ball went in.

"Nice shot, Milton," said Charlie, "but you're still traveling. You need to dribble. We'll have to work on that."

As the game went on, Ruthie recorded the strengths and weaknesses of the team. Once the game ended, she and Charlie made the team do fifteen minutes of drills. For the next couple of days, the gang practiced very hard and consistently reviewed the tapes of each of their practices. They were very confident they were ready for their first game, which was swiftly approaching.

The gang was eager to settle the score so that silent lunch would be terminated and they could go back to enjoying fun times with their peers at lunch. Since extracurricular activities had been canceled and silent lunch was such a drag, the gang enjoyed their basketball practices. It gave them a sense of hope.

Finally, the day they all had been waiting for arrived...game day! That morning, the gang met in their usual spot. Everyone was hyped to play.

"You guys, I'm so nervous and excited at the same time," said Ruthie. "However, we need to keep in mind that Pitts is going to try to take us out of our comfort zone by doing something stupid. So, Bustah and Petey, please, please keep that in mind. We have to keep our cool. Otherwise, we don't stand a chance."

"Yeah," chimed in Diego. "When we get mad, we don't think."

Suddenly, Pitts and his friends walked pass the gang. "Well, looky looky, it's the loser caboose!" he said as he patted Bustah on the head.

With a grimace, Buster jerked his head away from Pitts, and doing his best to remember what Ruthie told him about his temper, he swallowed his pride and remained quiet.

Pitts looked at Buster with a puzzled look. "What's wrong, Bus, rat got your licker?" He chuckled.

Suddenly, Diego got in Pitts's face. "Hey, mane, ball more. Talk less. We'll see you on the court, where we plan to leave your licker. So paso."

Pitts frowned. "Oh yeah. I predict your faces will be on the floor by the second quarter. By then, we'll have a twenty-point lead." He purposely stepped on Bustah's toe and walked off.

"What a basset hound of an idiot," said Charlie.

Ruthie looked over at Bustah, who was fuming on the inside and trying to keep it together on the outside. Suddenly, she reached out and grabbed him. "Bustah, I am so proud of you for keepin' your cool and not giving Pitts the satisfaction. You did so good that after the game, I'm buying you your own personal pizza. I know keeping cool isn't an easy thing, but you did it."

Bustah shook his head and smirked bashfully.

"But here's the best part," said Petey. "You get to take that aggression out on the court. You did it, Bus. Bus! Bus! Bus!"

The rest of the gang chimed in: "Bus! Bus! Bus! Soon, all the students in the surrounding area were chanting, "Bus! Bus! Bus!" It really gave Bustah a boost of confidence.

Everyone's cheers and Ruthie's inspirational words kept him pumped throughout the day, and he was more than ready for the game when school let out.

Chapter 6

After school, it was game time, and everyone headed to the gym. The gang stood outside to have a last-minute pep talk before going in.

"You guys," said Ruthie, "this is the first game. Remember, we have to win two out of three. We've practiced hard. More than anything, let's go out there and have fun. We know what we're up against and who we're dealing with, so expect some pushing, tripping, and shoving from Pitts's team. It's inevitable."

"Inevitable, what's that?" asked Milton.

"It means we can't avoid it, Milt."

"Oh."

"So, when they behave this way," said Ruthie, "don't be shocked. Keep your head in the game."

"We can do this. Stay strong," said Charlie. "'Bully who, respect the crew' on three."

They all put their hands out in the huddle, one on top of the other.

"One, two, three," said Ruthie.

"Bully who? Respect the Crew!" they shouted.

Ruthie led the team inside the gym. They walked in with savage game faces, ready to get down to business. The gym was pretty quiet, empty of fans since this was a private matter. Mr. Funkberry was standing in the center of the court with his metallic purple, gold, and white striped referee shirt and purple bell bottom dress pants. A white headband with basketballs on it surrounded his huge glistening afro.

"Hey, little warriors, hope ya got something good for us," he said as he rolled the basketball up and down his arms and across his back. "Y'all betta have come to slay as you play, or you'll end up in disarray. Keep your head in the game, and you should see good results that will bring you fame."

"Cool, Unc Funk! Thanks for the advice, amigo," said Diego.

"Come on, you guys. Let's warm up," said Ruthie.

While the gang warmed up, Pitts and his crew walked into the gym. "Well, look what we have here. If it isn't the booger busters. Are y'all ready to get tore out the frame?!"

The whole time Pitts and his crew talked trash, Ruthie anxiously stared at Petey and Bustah, hoping they remembered the conversation from earlier about not allowing Pitts to ruffle their feathers. Bustah was trying desperately not to say anything, and Pitts knew it.

"What's wrong, Buuuuus?! You look like an angry toilet that's about to get fluuuushed!" The rest of his crew laughed hysterically.

Mr. Funkberry blew his whistle. "It's game time in five minutes, so today, we shall see who's going to win it."

"Alright, you guys, let's huddle," said Charlie. "We've got this, guys! Remember, keep your head in the game, and Milton, no traveling! Pudge, we're going to need you to move down the court faster than normal. Milton, put your game face on. Don't let Pitts and his clones intimidate you. With this army, there's no need to be scared."

"You're going to do great, Milton," said Bustah.

His compliment took Milton's confidence level from zero to five in a matter of seconds. Bustah was one of the popular kids at school, and he was always highly conscious of the influence he had on people. He knew that people listened to every word he said and took it for a rainbow full of Skittles. Aware of his power, he always felt it was his job to encourage the unpopular and diffident students who were clueless about their place on the social spectrum.

"Alright, let's do this!" said Charlie as the game-time buzzer blew.

Finally, it was showtime. Both teams huddled in their respective places for tip-off. Mr. Funkberry stood in the middle.

"Alright, little termites, it's time to put up a fight. For once, we'll settle the score of who's wrong and who's right. Let's play fair now. It's all in fun, and there's no need for one to kick the other when they're down. There'll be no hitting or swearing when you get upset. Persevering through the pain will be your best bet. That way, you don't have to worry about being a reject of the game and be forced off this court with your head down in shame. We all want the same, to play a cool, clean, funktastic game. Isn't that right?! Now, howl if you're with me and growl if you're against me."

Everyone howled in agreement. The echoing howls bounced off the walls as Mr. Funkberry threw the ball up in the air.

Pitts tipped the ball over to his side of the court, and his buddy dribbled it down to the other end and slam dunked the ball into the hoop. Pudge grabbed the ball and dribbled quickly down the court, passing the ball to Diego, who was wide open for a nice jump shot. Pitts grabbed the ball and started to dribble down the court, but it wasn't as easy as he thought it would be as Bustah was on him like skin on taters. Pitts leaped and attempted to release the ball to his buddy, but Bustah interjected himself, strong-armed the ball from Pitts, and passed it to Petey, who laid up the shot for the lead.

Pitts's face began to flare up with irritation as he tried to remain calm. Once again, his buddy had the ball. He dribbled quickly down the court and leaped for a nice jump shot. Bustah grabbed the ball and coasted down the court. As he bounced the ball, his eyes were fixated on Milton and Charlie, who were nearby, while his mind was fixated on the number fifty. First team to fifty would win. Currently, the score was twenty-five to twenty-seven. This was the perfect time to pass the ball to Milton since he was closer to the basket than Charlie and was guarded by a weak blocker.

After faking out Pitts, Bustah passed the ball to Milton with a backhand release. Milton caught it, and swoosh! Bustah smiled at Milton and pointed his finger at him as if to say, *You're the man.* Milton's confidence inflated just a bit more.

"Nice job, Milton!" yelled Ruthie.

Back and forth, the two teams played, neither side giving an inch, but then Pitt's team started to pull ahead. When they hit a few jump shots in a row, Ruthie signaled to Mr. Funkberry that they needed a time out.

"We're doing great, you guys," she said, but Pudge I need you to get down the court faster to be able to get those rebounds. Diego, I need you to put pressure on Pitts. Bustah and Charlie, I need you to distract him. I'm noticing that they're dependent on Pitts and his lieutenant, so we need to capitalize on this weakness. Milt, remember, no traveling. We have twenty-eight points to go. Keep your head in the game, everybody. 'Bully who?' on three. One, two, three. Bully who?"

"Respect the crew!" screamed the team.

The team headed back on the court. Pitts's team had possession. On their next three plays, though, they missed all their shots. Two of the rebounds were grabbed by Pudge and one by Milton, and they scored at the other end on all three possessions. This tied the game at thirty-eight.

As Pitt's team became desperate to pull ahead, their physical aggression towards the gang caused them to foul Bustah and Milton each time they went up for a shot. Milton missed all his free throws, but Bustah, being the determined, competitive person that he is, hit all five of his. Now the gang was ahead forty-three to thirty-eight.

Pitts hit a massive three pointer and was fouled by Charlie. His two free throws at the foul line were successful. The score was tied again: forty-three to forty-three. This made the hairs on Petey's back stand up. Looking at how exhausted Bustah, Charlie, and Pudge were, he knew he had to step up and do something. He called for a time out.

"Look, you guys," he said. "Milton and Diego, it's time for us to pick up the slack. We have to win this game. Milton, you make better shots when you're closer to the basket, so stay near it and be ready. Diego, I need you to block the lieutenant, and everyone else, block like crazy, but please try not to foul them. Bus, you ready?"

"Let's do it."

One, two, three... Bully who?" yelled Petey.

"Respect the crew," they shouted.

Ruthie beamed from ear to ear, proud of how Petey taken the initiative and stepped up during what seemed to be desperate times.

Petey grabbed the ball and passed it to Pudge, who, with all his might, pressed through the fatigue, sped down the court for a fast break, and hammered the shot home.

The lieutenant had the ball, but as he dribbled down the court, Milton was all over him, making sure he was unable to get it to the basket. If Milton had never defended himself against a bully, his elevated defensive skills were now making up for it. The lieutenant released the ball into the air, and Petey and Milton both smacked it away from him. Everyone scurried toward the ball in panic. Pitts leaped into the air and snatched it up.

"Nooo!" Petey screamed as he ran down the court after Pitts, who had pulled up at the three-point line to make a shot.

As Pitts released the ball, a scrawny kid leaped as high as he could and scraped it off the rim. He passed the ball to Diego.

"Way to go, Milton!" shouted Ruthie. "That's the spirit!"

Diego leaped high and released the ball at the three-point line, and swish!

Just two more, Bustah said to himself.

Suddenly, a surge of energy emerged once more inside of him just as he was trying to block Pitts from receiving a pass that was bound to come his way. The lieutenant passed the ball, and Bustah quickly intercepted it and hit a fadeaway jump shot to win the game.

71

The gang cheered loud and proud. Ruthie ran on the court and yanked Bustah by the neck, happily wrestling him to the floor. Bustah, who was tickled, was also trying to escape her takedown.

"Bully who?!" she yelled repeatedly in his ear.

"Alright already," he said, chuckling.

She happily got up and ran to Petey. "Bully who?!" she said loudly and in a deep voice.

"Respect the crew!" Petey yelled back.

They carried on with their hooting and hollering for about five minutes. Meanwhile, Pitts was on the other end of the court, yelling and screaming at his team.

Bustah mustered up the humility to walk over and encourage them. "Good job, you guys! You were a great match."

"Thanks, Bustah," said the lieutenant and two other teammates.

Pitts stormed in Bustah's face with anger. "Great match? What a load of crap! Your crappy team of basketball rejects can't even compare. Don't celebrate too hard, because, at the next game, your hind is hammered," he said as he pounded his right fist into his left hand.

Bustah fixed his mouth to say something very hurtful, but then he turned and glanced over at how happy his team was. He realized that this game was bigger than he and Pitts's personal beef with one another. He also understood that there was no need to argue with Pitts, because, that afternoon, the brigade had reigned victorious. He looked at Pitts and said, "Good game, man," and walked off to continue celebrating with his team.

Mr. Funkberry walked over to the winning team and gave each member a high five on the backhand side. "That game was tight, lil' dynamites, but focus, focus, focus 'cause there's another one Wednesday night. I'm out of sight. Peace." With that, Mr. Funkberry strolled smoothly out of the gym with his basketball rotating on one finger.

After much celebration, Ruthie treated the gang to pizza at Luigi's, and then they called it a night. She gave them the following day off, but the day after, they were back on the court doing the same drills from before and working on jump shots.

Milton stood at the free throw line. He bounced the ball twice, bent his knees, and sent the ball up and into the net.

"Swish!" he said.

"Way to go, Milton!" said Diego. "That's the fifth one in a row. Now, if you can do that, then you can make foul shots during the games."

"No, I can't," said Milton.

"Yes, you can.".

"But whenever I try to make the foul shot in the game, my palms and back get sweaty like a grease monkey, or I start to feel like the drips of water on a boiling hot pot."

Diego chuckled. "Well, amigo, did you know dat when you're nervous like dat, you have, ahhh…how do you say…more power?" Think about el carro. When you crank up, ah, de power, it cause car, ah, zoom zoom. Just like car when it cranks but gets crunk when nervous, meaning it has to go."

"Go as in fart?" said Milton.

"Ha-ha-ha! No, cucaracha! Go as in run. It means dat your juices are flowing and you have power to make your body do what you want. You're in control, remember dat. When I get dat way, I scream like this." Diego screamed, "Aaaaaah!" as he shook his head from side to side and ran in place. "Or I do this." He twitched his body as if he were being electrocuted, rapidly jerking his chest in and out and falling to the pavement.

He popped back up. "Then I conquer my fears. You should try it sometime, mane."

Milton laughed uncontrollably at Diego's antics. Once the laughter subsided, a moment of gloom seeped into his heart and covered his face. Suddenly, he felt awful as he thought about how nice the gang had been to him and how they had welcomed him with open arms. This was his first time getting to know the gang, and they had already done so much for him mentally and physically that he felt he could never repay them.

"Que pasa?" asked Diego. "Why you look so sad? You were just laughing."

"No reason. Just grateful for you guys."

"Oh, we grateful for you, mane. You represent one more life we get to change. I know it's tough for you being picked on and bullied. People don't understand what that does to a kid. Especially if you don't have anyone to vent to or that will protect you at home. But just know that there's nothing wrong wit' standing up for yourself. Even if you get hurt doing it, at least you didn't go down without a fight or without trying. You're second to none. Once you realize that, you'll survive."

Suddenly, Milton began crying. "I feel so sorry that you guys have to put up with me."

"Hey, hey, easy, amigo! You're no burden. We want to help. So, cheer up."

One great thing about Diego was that he was a good voice of reason. On the outside, he looked extremely self-centered, but once you peeled off the cool black leather jacket and shades he faithfully wore, you got to enjoy the perks of a peer counselor. Everyone knew Diego as the nonchalant party starter who seemed to not have a care in the world. A lot of students at Misfit Elementary wished they had his personality. But if only they'd known his story...

Chapter 7

After another grueling week of practice, it was time for game two. Once again, the gang walked onto the gym floor, but this time, they were accompanied by a few fans. Apparently, a few of Pitts's teammates had been so irritatingly impressed by the gang's last performance that the news of it had spread around the school, and some people were eager to witness another epic defeat.

"Ooooooh myy gooosh!" said Charlie, shocked by the small crowd of people.

"This is so unexpected," said Pudge.

As both teams warmed up, they noticed an unfamiliar face approaching them on the court, an older man about five-feet-ten-inches tall with broad shoulders, a full orange beard, and a baseball cap.

"Who is that guy?" asked Pudge.

"Good afternoon, kids!" the man said when he got close to the group. "Mr. Funkberry had an emergency, so he won't make it tonight. I've been assigned to coach the game tonight."

"Is Mr. Funkberry okay?" asked Petey.

"Yeah, he's fine. He had a situation with a family member that he needed to handle."

Petey gasped a sigh of relief. "Oh, okay. You almost scared me to death."

"I'm Coach Dandy, by the way. We'll start in five minutes."

"Okay, thanks," said Pudge.

As soon as Coach Dandy walked away, the gang groaned and moaned heavily.

"Boy, if this ain't a monkey wrench," said Charlie.

They huddled together.

"Alright, guys, we gotta take care of business," said Charlie.

"'Bully who?' on three. One, two, three," said Ruthie.

"Bully who? Respect the crew!" they yelled in unison.

Coach Dandy blew the whistle, and both teams got in position, ready for tip-off. He blew the whistle again and threw the ball straight up in the air.

Pitts aggressively slapped it to his end of the court. He quickly passed the ball to his lieutenant. The lieutenant went for a layup and put the first two points on the board.

Charlie picked up the rebound and dribbled quickly down the court. As she jumped and released the ball, Pitts stole it away and hustled down the court for a fast break and a swish.

Pudge quickly grabbed the ball and hustled down the court. He passed the ball to Bustah, who was wide open, and Bustah tossed the ball in the basket for a deuce.

Coach Dandy gave Pitts a stern look. "Get it together, Andy!" he yelled.

For the next seven possessions, Pudge and Petey were double-teaming Pitts something awful, stealing the ball away and forcing missed shots, and Bustah, Charlie, and Diego were milking every minute of it at the other end. They were hot. Coach Dandy was trying his best to keep cool, but once the gang's seventh shot connected, his face started turning red, his voice went from calm to frantic, and he called a time-out.

"Andy! what in the pigeon poop is wrong with ya'?" he yelled as his head vibrated up and down. "A team captain shouldn't allow his man to be that open. You better toughen up! You're playin' stupid. Stupid! Stupid! Stupid!" he said as his body swayed back and forth.

"Now, strengthen your defense and play like ya came to win. You're already down twelve points. You better not ever let them scrawny little birds hem you up like that again. That's a darn shame. They're half your size. Don't embarrass me, boy!"

Wait a minute! Why is Coach Dandy coaching Andy if he's the referee for the night? Thought Charlie.

"Alright, let's get back in the game," said Ruthie. 'Bully who?' on three."

"Bully who? Respect the crew!" said the team.

As Pitts and the team approached the court, a look of redemption shined ever so brightly on his face. Coach Dandy blew the whistle, and the final minutes of the first quarter began.

Once again, Pudge and Petey were putting pressure on Pitts. The lieutenant threw him the ball, and he caught it and elbowed Petey in the face as he made a fadeaway jump shot.

"Foul!" Petey said as he held his bruised cheek in his hands.

"That wasn't a foul," said Coach Dandy.

"Yes, it was," said Petey.

"Mind your manners, boy, and shake it off."

Petey rolled his eyes and walked away. As the game continued, the brigade endured three quarters of bad and blown calls by Coach Dandy! When the final game-ending whistle was blown, Pitts and his team screamed and shouted like little hooligans over their biased victory, while the gang looked on with vengeance in their eyes.

Now that the series was tied, they knew they had one more shot left, and they were more motivated than ever to fight for the win. As Charlie watched Pitts and his team cheer and Coach Dandy give Pitts a high five, she couldn't help but replay Coach Dandy's comment during the first quarter: *Don't embarrass me, boy! Don't embarrass me, boy!*

The comment played constantly in her mind as she followed everyone else outside, and she kept staring at Coach Dandy's and Pitts's heads as they bobbed up and down while the two were talking. Then it happened... Coach Dandy removed his red trucker's hat from his head, revealing a shock of wavy honey blonde hair that was identical to Pitts's.

"Oh, you guys! Coach Dandy is Andy's dad!" she screamed as she ran full force through the crowd to catch up with them.

"Wait, what?" said Diego. He put two and two together and ran after Charlie.

Suddenly, the rest of the gang caught on and took off running after Charlie as well. "Nooooooo, Charlie!" they all yelled.

"You toilet lickers! You jipped us!" Charlie shouted while running at full speed.

Pitts and Coach Dandy looked back, saw the brigade sprinting towards them, and they sped off laughing. "Losers!" yelled Pitts, holding up the letter L with his right hand as his dad stuck his tongue out at the gang and wrinkled up his nose.

"We've been bamboozled, you guys!" said Charlie.

Diego began stroking his chin, pondering. "If he was the referee, then what really happened to Mr. Funkberry?"

"Yeah, we need to see if Mr. Funkberry knew about this," said Pudge. "

"That's an answer we won't get until Monday, you guys," said Ruthie. "In the meantime, let's go to my house."

She knew just what the gang needed at a time like this. When the gang reached her house, she went to her closet and pulled out a yellow, green, and blue pack of tape. She placed yellow tape on the floor in a zig-zag, red tape in curvy lines, and green tape in a straight line.

"What is this, some game?" Pudge asked.

"Yep. Alright, guys, choose teams," Ruthie instructed. "Choose a color and walk the line. The first round is practice. The next round is a contest."

Pudge, Charlie, and Diego were one team, and Bustah, Milton, and Petey were on the other.

"Oh, this is a piece of cake," said Pudge.

"Yeah, it is," said Bustah.

"Of course," said Petey, "because it's the first round."

Milton was the last person to walk the line. After he did, Ruthie pulled out two blindfolds.

"Let the fun begin!" she yelled.

The gang looked puzzled. "Wait a minute, what's the point of this game, Ruthie?" asked Bustah.

"Stop asking questions and just have fun," she replied. "Ok, teams, go ahead and pick who will be blindfolded. Hmm, on second thought, I'll do it."

Ruthie knew this game was about patience and listening to your partner, so she chose to blindfold the two weakest links: Charlie and Bustah. They were so used to giving directions that she decided to take them out of their comfort zone by flipping the script.

"Bustah and Charlie, you are going to walk the zig-zag line, and your teammates are going to guide you to the finish line. This means you guys have to listen to their directions."

"We better not lose," said Bustah.

"Oh, shut ya potty hole," said Charlie. "You guys lost already 'cause everyone knows Bustah don't like takin' orders."

"Get in your places, people," said Ruthie. "On your mark, get set, go!"

At that point, all Charlie and Bustah could hear were voices shouting, telling them to move to the right and the left, and sometimes, they ended up following the other team's directions.

Ultimately, Charlie's team won. Once they took her blindfold off and she saw that Bustah was still trying to get to the finish line, she yelled in a deep voice, "Yes, Bustah! I beat you! Bustah you got bussed up!" Everyone laughed, including Bustah.

"That was fun, Ruthie!" Pudge said with a chuckle.

"Thanks. I'm glad you guys enjoyed it. Now, Bus, what was the point of the game?"

"Well," he replied, "I started getting frustrated in the beginning because my teammates were confusing me, and then I had to tell myself to stay calm, listen, and see it through. So, I would have to say it taught me that I need to be more patient and listen more when others are trying to tell me things."

"Yeah, me too," Charlie agreed. "It really taught me patience. Because I was like, if the person with the stinky breath yell out left or right one mo' time, I'm gone need CPR."

The gang chuckled so hard. "Just kidding," Charlie said with a giggle.

Chapter 8

Monday morning, before the first bell rang, the gang busted into Mr. Funkberry's classroom.

"Mr. Funkberry!" they all yelled in unison.

"Why didn't you tell us that Andy's dad was refereeing the game in your absence last week?" asked Charlie.

"Yeah, uh huh," said Diego.

Mr. Funkberry, so calm and cool, took three slow sips of his coffee before responding. "Good morning, kiddo diddos! My heart is weak because you hustled and bustled in here and did not speak. I love you guys like crazy, but your intro was bleak."

But Mr. Funkberry, you had to..."

Mr. Funkberry placed his long finger over his huge lips. "Shhh! Let's try this again, my friends. Walk back out and come back in. Then we can begin."

The gang mumbled and grumbled as they dragged their feet back outside. They pushed the door open slowly this time. "Good morning, Mr. Funkberry. How are you today?" they said.

"I'm great. What brings you here, panting deer?"

"We want to know if you knew that Andy's dad refereed the game on Friday?" asked Charlie.

"What! No! No! Nobody told me so! The janitor Mr. Lee was supposed to fill in for me! Hmmm! Doesn't this seem like a conspiracy?!"

Surprising everyone, Mr. Lee entered the classroom. "Good morning! Today is your lucky day,

Mr. Funkberry. The bulb for your projector finally came in."

"Great news, but have a seat, 'cause I'm 'bout to stew," warned Mr. Funkberry.

A puzzled look clouded Mr. Lee's face. "What's going on?"

"My mane, why didn't you referee the game?"

"Well, Mr. Pitts offered me fifty bucks to take my place."

"Isn't this some knee-jerkin' jive? Your only job was to hold it down and keep it live. You know we can't trust Mr. Pitts, the same man that pouts when, for him, the situation doesn't fit. You owe these kids an apology because, out of them, Pitts made a mockery."

"I'm truly sorry, you guys," said Mr. Lee. "I didn't know how much the game meant to you. Please forgive me." He smiled. "I tell ya what. On Thursday, the basketball team won't have practice. So, what do you think about occupying the space for one of your practices?"

"Cool, alright!" they yelled.

"Muy bueno, Mr. Lee," said Diego.

"It's the least I could do," said Mr. Lee.

The bell rang, and the gang went to their homeroom classes. Ruthie, Petey, and Pudge entered Mrs. Goozerbee's class. She grabbed her yardstick from the whiteboard and began whacking her desk with it. "Let's go!" Whack! "Let's go! I'm ready to start." Whack! Whack!

The students scrambled to get their notebooks and materials off the shelf and hurried to their seats.

"Hustle! Hustle! We don't have all day. Open your books to page fifty-two. Today, we're learning fractions. Before I begin, I need you to write down what you see here on the board and the common errors students make when learning fractions. You have ten minutes."

As Petey got started, he realized that he'd forgotten to get a pencil from his bookbag. He knew not to ask Mrs. Goozerbee since that would mean that he had violated one of her rules: be prepared for class. He began to sweat frantically because he knew that if he didn't find a pencil quick, he would be pot roast. Petey yawned, stretched his arms behind him, and attempted to delicately pick up a pencil off Penny Proudfoot's desk. His hand had barely left Penny's desk when she pounced on it with her fist.

"Ouch!" he yelled.

Knowing that Mrs. Goozerbee would flip out, Penny yelled, "Petey, don't you dare try to steal my pencil! It's not my fault you didn't bring your own. Next time, come prepared."

Petey gave Penny the most wicked grimace one could witness. Mrs. Goozerbee came storming over to his desk, and she hit it with the yardstick. Whack! Petey jumped.

"Why are you bothering Ms. Proudfoot, and how come you don't have all of your materials?" she yelled.

"I do, but I forgot to get my pencil out of my bookbag," he replied.

"You forgot! Well, son, you won't forget about this detention that you just earned," she said.

Penny smirked and let out a light giggle.

"You think this is funny, Ms. Proudfoot?" said Mrs. Goozerbee. "Oh, you have no idea how thin the ice is between me and you."

"I didn't do anything," said Penny.

Whack! "Are you talking back to me girl?!"

"No, I'm just telling you that I didn't do anything."

"That's talking back, popcorn jaws! Both of you have detention and lunch duty today with Ms. Kaufmann."

"Oh gosh!" they both moaned. Petey slumped down in his chair with his arms crossed over his chest. Penny kicked his chair in frustration.

"Let me dial her extension right now," said Mrs. Goozerbee.

All Petey could think about was how he wouldn't be able to sit with the gang during lunch even if they were still having silent lunches.

Towards the end of class, Mrs. Goozerbee wrote Petey and Penny a hall pass to go see Ms. Kaufmann. In the cafeteria kitchen, there stood an amazingly tall old lady with multiple ear piercings and white spiky hair molded like a shark fin at the crown of her head. "The infamous Penny," she said with a wicked smile. "So, you're back again. I assume you want to be a cafeteria manager just like me when you grow up. If only I loved spending so much time with you as you enjoy spending with me."

Her smile abruptly changed into a snarl. "Get to mixin'," she said as she slammed the bowl on the counter. She turned to Petey with a strange look on her face.

"Well, if this isn't your first time, then hopefully, it'll be your last," she said as she yanked him by the collar with her left hand and pointed a wooden spatula dripping with fish stick batter in his face with the other. Petey looked horrified.

"Don't let me catch you in here again, newbie." She raised her eyebrows. "Go stock the cutlery before the booger babies arrive!"

Under her watchful scowl, and with fear in his eyes, Petey began stocking the cutlery tray. Three minutes later, Milton entered the kitchen with his cheeks drooping down past his chin. Ms. Kaufman served him a piercing squint and yelled, "Go help Penny!"

He immediately grabbed the large tin bowl and began moving his left arm in a rapid circular motion. Petey gave Milton a puzzled stare. He couldn't understand why such a good kid was on lunch duty. *What could he have possibly done?* he wondered.

Ms. Kaufmann walked over to Penny and Milton. "That's enough! Go get ready to serve!" she yelled. The two rushed over to the food service line while Ms. Kaufman fried the fish sticks. As Petey was stocking cutlery, fruit, and milk, he could see that there was some verbal and physical friction between the other two kids. Penny subtly bumped her hip into Milton's. "You better do it, Mopy Milton," she whispered, "or else I'll tell everyone about how you peed all over yourself last summer at camp because you were scared of a baby turtle."

Petey could see that Milton was in distress, as his cheeks turned red and swelled with air and he took heavy, irritated breaths. *What is she forcing him to do?* he wondered.

Suddenly, the clinking and clanking of a metal pot got everyone's attention. "Alright, you guys, the booger babies are coming right about now!" said Ms.

Kaufman. Suddenly, the classes began coasting through the lunch line.

"Fish sticks, or macaroni?" Penny had to repeat multiple times. While she loaded mac and cheese and fish sticks on lunch trays, Petey passed out the fruit, and Milton served the steamed broccoli and cornbread.

As the flow of traffic in the line winded down, Bustah and Charlie strolled through the line. They locked eyes with Petey, and before he could explain, they said in unison, "We know."

"Catch ya later, bro!" said Bustah. As Penny placed the mac and cheese on Charlie's tray, Charlie looked daggers at her. She stuck out her tongue and rolled her eyes behind Charlie's back. Bustah greeted Penny with a sly grin, and as she reached over to place the scooped-up fish sticks on his tray, he purposely moved his tray just in time for them to fall on the counter.

"I don't like what you're serving," he said. "Something's very fishy."

Penny rolled her eyes in disgust. Then she realized that Bustah was the last person in line. "Okay, you guys," she said. "We can make our plates now. We're done."

Ms. Kauffman closed one of the food service line doors, emptied the cash register, and locked herself in her office so that she could count the profit for the day. Penny, Milton, and Petey wolfed down their lunches quietly, as they all knew that they only had five minutes to eat before they had to go back to class.

Penny stared at Petey with a smile. "Petey, I'm sorry for getting you in trouble this morning. I was having a bad morning. My baby sister spilled milk all over my favorite sweater, and I was livid! I shouldn't have taken it out on you." She extended her balled fist out towards Petey, and he reluctantly connected his with hers.

"Let's get ready to collect the lunch trays," she continued. "Petey, can you go in the side room on the left and get the garbage bag and place it in the garbage container so that we can start collecting trays? Actually, you can go ahead and get the left side of the cafeteria. We'll take the right side. Come on, Milton. Let's go."

"I don't want to," Milton replied.

"We have to do it," said Penny in a demonic voice.

Milton stomped out of the kitchen and into the side room. The garbage bags, trash cans, and cleaning supplies were stored in rooms on the left and right side of the kitchen. As soon as Petey left the kitchen, she grabbed Milton by the hand and stuffed a few fish sticks in his pocket and hers. Then she handed him two apples, folded her shirt over like a makeshift basket, and tossed in five apples. They ran toward the side room opposite the one Petey was in.

This side room was a little different than the one Petey had entered. In one wall was a charcoal-gray-tinted sliding window. It offered a panoramic view of a silent crowd eating in misery because of an unsuspected, self-absorbed perpetrator who relished in devious activity.

Penny Proudfoot placed the apples that she had tucked into her shirt onto the peach wooden counter in front of the window and slid the window back. The mobile blackboard normally used for tic-tac-toe or hangman stood five feet in front of the window. It easily masked their identity. Penny peered carefully around the blackboard to ensure that the security monitors were not paying attention. One of them sat on his brown wooden stool, eating an apple and reading a book. The other paced up and down the middle aisle, making sure that there wasn't a peep heard from the students.

"Alright," she whispered in a cunning voice, "Milton, shoot!"

She began throwing apples and fish sticks across the cafeteria. One of them smacked the security guard in the back, and once again, pandemonium erupted as the kids who fell victim to Penny's shenanigans began rattling mac and cheese across the room.

Meanwhile, after diligently looking for trash bags, Petey entered the kitchen to the sounds of screaming and mayhem. *What's going on?* he thought as he searched the other side of the kitchen for Penny to ask her where the trash bags were. He looked around the kitchen and couldn't find her. He noticed a crack in the side room door, and as he opened it, to his surprise, Penny, with Milton beside her, was swiftly darting fish sticks across the cafeteria at the students.

"I don't want to do this!" said Milton.

"Do it, or I'll tell your secret," said Penny.

In shock and disbelief, Petey took out his cell phone and videotaped Penny throwing food. "I gotcha now," he said.

Suddenly, Penny turned around, and that devious smile of excitement turned to mush as she realized she was being recorded.

107

"So, you're the reason we're having silent lunch?" Petey asked.

"I can explain."

"Oh, sure you will."

"Stop! Stop it!" she whined as she began to panic. "Cut that thing off. Please, I'll do whatever you want as long as my mother doesn't find out about this. Please! Please!".

Milton looked on with a sigh of relief. He was happy that the torture had finally come to a halt.

After deciding that he had recorded enough information, Petey paused the recording, placed his phone in his cargo pants, and secured it by buttoning the pocket. He was determined to make sure this proof of evidence was stored and secured safely for the powers that be if needed.

"Penny, do you realize how much trouble you've caused? Why would you put the entire school's freedom in jeopardy? You have everything that you want. I don't understand."

Penny's red, puffy eyes began to swell with tears. "Since my baby sister, Charlotte, was born, my mom and dad don't have time to take me to the park. My mom and I haven't gone to get pedicures in, like, six months. We normally go twice a month. My feet look like alligator skin. See?" She reached down and removed her left white sock and canvas sneaker.

Petey laughed. "Are you serious? It's really not that bad."

"It's not funny. My whole world has been turned over since Charlotte was born. Every time she cries, our plans get put on hold. Every time she laughs or rolls around, everyone thinks it's just so cute and funny. Well, I'm cute and funny too! I just want things to go back the way they were."

"And they will," said Petey, once you get over yourself. I think there's enough love to be shared between the two of you. Look, they're not giving her more attention because they love her more. She's getting more attention because she can't talk, walk, dress, and feed herself like you can."

Penny's mood went from gloomy to slightly cheerful. "I never thought of it that way. Thanks," she said as she sniffled.

Petey gave Milton a puzzled stare. "I thought you said Pitts was bullying you and that he was behind all of this."

"Well, it wasn't Pitts. It was Penny the whole time."

"Then why would you lie?" asked Petey.

"Because if I told, she said she would tell everyone my secret," said Milton.

"I understand that you were scared, Milton," Petey yelled, "but do you know how much time and energy we've wasted with these basketball games, and Pitts isn't even the culprit?"

He thought for a moment. "Okay, so this is how this is going to go. Penny, you're playing this last basketball game against Pitts with my crew. Milton, you're going to apologize to Pitts."

"What?!" said Milton.

"Suck it up and own it," said Petey. We owe him an apology too, so you're not alone. I'm not going to expose this video, but if you don't tell the principal the whole truth and nothing but the truth, I will. Today is Monday. So, I'll give you until Wednesday to get yourself together or write a letter to the principal explaining what you did. If I don't see any changes in the cafeteria by Friday, it means that you were a coward and didn't follow my orders. Then you'll be exposed. I gotta go. Practice starts at three tomorrow. Be there."

Chapter 9

Petey was extremely anxious to share with the gang what he had just witnessed. He quickly texted: *Code red meet me by the oak tree after school.*

The bell rang, and the students came flying out of the classrooms, thoroughly happy to be released. Petey wasted no time tackling the back door and rushing out to the oak tree to meet the crew. He was so excited to share this juicy information with them, and how he had accidentally solved the case. As he waited, he paced back and forth with excitement. Then he spotted the crew heading towards him.

"Alright, what's going on?" said Bustah with undertones of concern.

"Guys! You will never believe this! Guess who is responsible for the lunchroom disasters?"

With puzzled faces, they all said in unison, "Who? "

"Wait, it's Pitts, of course! duh!" said Charlie.

"No," Petey proudly stated. "It's Penny and Milton."

"What?!" Charlie shouted. Her top lip curled with a cringe as she stood with her hands on her hips.

"Espera, hombre!" said Diego. "You mean to tell me we wasted all dat time trying to help him and he's been in on this the whole time?".

"No, it's not what you think," said Petey. "Apparently, there's something Penny's holding over his head, and she blackmailed him into starting food fights in the cafeteria."

"Ahh, I see," said Diego.

"And how did you catch them?" asked Pudge.

"We all had cafeteria duty because Penny got me in trouble," Petey explained, "and she asked me to collect the trays on the left side of the cafeteria. I couldn't find the trash bags, so I walked to the right side of the room to ask her to show me where they were, and there her and Milton were, firing mac and cheese out the side window."

"But," said Ruthie, "how could she be the culprit when, a few weeks back, she got hit with a taco and went ballistic...remember?"

"That's a good question. Let's ask Milton," said Bustah.

Milton was anxiously walking towards them with his head down. He tried to pretend as if he did not see them as he attempted to pass right by them. Bustah grabbed his book bag.

"Milton."

"Huh?" He jumped.

"Did you start the first food fight in the cafeteria?"

'Yes," he said nervously, "but only because Penny made me do it."

Bustah noticed that Milton was breathing rapidly and obviously scared. "It's okay, Milton. We know you didn't do this intentionally. Actually, it's all starting to make sense."

"Go home and relax, Milton," said Charlie. "It's all good and free of charge."

"I'm sorry, you guys," said Milton as he walked off.

"Any who," said Petey, "I told Penny that she has to confess to the principal by Friday, or else. Oh, I almost forgot. I caught it all on video." He pulled out his black cellphone, hit play, and the gang watched in shock as Penny went to work making everyone look like sloppy seconds.

"I gotta give it to ya, Petey," said Pudge. "This is good stuff."

"Oh yeah!" said Ruthie.

Petey continued. "I also told her and Milton that they both have to apologize to Pitts and that she has to help us finish what we started. So, she'll be at our next practice."

"Really?" asked Bustah. "I don't know if I like the idea of her being on our team, especially with us trying to win."

"At this point, amigo," said Diego, "it's not about us and Pitts. It's really about her, Milton, and Pitts. So, maybe Pitts should take Penny, and we'll keep Milton.".

"Done deal," said Petey.

"You know, guys, this means that we might be doing his homework," said Charlie.

"Well, we still owe him an apology," said Petey. "And we have to own that."

"Yep, you're right.".

"When's the next game again?" asked Pudge.

"Next Wednesday," said Charlie.

"Gotta make sure we talk to Andy ASAP and tell him that we need him to take Penny."

"Okay, so how about we talk to him tomorrow?" Ruthie suggested.

"Cool. Adios!" said Diego.

"See you guys tomorrow," said Ruthie.

The next morning, Ruthie spotted Pitts in the hallway by the cafeteria. "Hey, Pitts, you gotta minute?" she asked.

"What do you want, Pootie Ruthie?" he scoffed.

"How lame, cheater! That's all you've got?"

"Cheater? We won that game fair and square."

"Oh, it was fair and square, alright. You should feel busted and embarrassed since your daddy had to save you from a beatdown. Ooh, picture this headline, 'Sixth Grader Pitts Pulls Pitiful Stunt in Game Two by Having Daddy Secretly Come to His Rescue.'"

"Oh, shut it, Ruthie!"

"Anyways, we need to chat after school. Meet me at the gym."

"Yeah, whatever," said Pitts as he rolled his eyes and walked off.

When the final bell rang, Pitts met Ruthie and the gang in front of the gym. "I thought you were going to be alone, Ruthie," he said.

"Nope, you know we're one for all and all for one," Ruthie replied. "Look, Pitts, we apologize for accusing you of starting the food fight in the cafeteria."

Suddenly, a little voice said, "It's not their fault, Pitts. It's mine." Milton made his way to the front of the group. "I lied and told them that you were the one who was responsible for starting all of the food fights in the cafeteria when really it was Penny Proudfoot. I'm so sorry. I only did it because Penny was bullying me." His head drooped to the ground, and he thrust his hands in his pockets and stood on the sides of his feet and flexed them back and forth.

"We're sorry for thinking that you were behind this mess the whole time," said Bustah.

"Yeah," said Pudge.

"Lo siento, mane," said Diego.

"Yeah, we apologize," said Petey.

Pitts stood in awe...speechless. With his right index finger and thumb hugging his chin, he stared pensively into space.

"As much as I want my fist to kiss your faces," he finally said, "I have to say thank you. Don't get it twisted. I still loathe you dweebs, but I must say I have mad respect for you. No one has ever apologized to me for lying on me or accusing me of something I didn't do. That's pretty cool coming from the 'righteous crew,'" he added, making air quotes with his fingers.

"Wait," said Petey, "before we go any further, I think we need to show a bit more compassion for Penny."

"Why?" Charlie asked.

"The reason Penny started the food fights is because she's jealous of her baby sister and craving attention at home. Her mom will kill her if she finds out. Therefore, I was thinking of prepping her for her meeting with Principal Strongarm by suggesting she offer to do the charity game in lieu of the principal telling her parents about the horrible things she did.

"Really, Petey?" Charlie asked. "I'm going to have to say no on this one."

"Come on, Charlie. She's already in deep doody, so let's cut her some slack."

"Why? She's never cut us any slack. How is this going to hurt you?" Charlie rebelliously locked her arms across her chest and turned her back to Petey.

"It doesn't… My point exactly!" he exclaimed.

"After all the stress she caused us over the years, like the time she tripped ya durin' the cross-country race to win first place, or the time she wrote her name on Pudge's homework and turned it in as hers because she failed to complete the assignment and Pudge had to suffer with a failin' grade. Or what about when she threw Diego's bookbag on the school bus just as the bus driver was drivin' off because he beat her fair and square in the dance contest at recess? Is this the type of person we want to save? She does mo' damage than good, and if this situation was reversed, she wouldn't give a poopa' scoopa' about any of us. She would just simply say, 'Off with their heads.'"

"We have her on video," said Petey. "She's promoting this game all by herself, and she has to confess to the principal. What more do you want?"

"Her mama ta give her a good pop on the booty!" After a pause, and with a smile, Charlie added, "Nah, just kiddin'."

The crew giggled.

"Okay, okay, I guess she's suffered enough," Charlie confessed.

Charlie interjected, "Well, Pitts we were thinkin' that Penny could play on your team for the charity game and we'll keep Milton."

"Charity game? Oh, there won't be a charity game for us. We've already had our time wasted. Here's the plan. Milton, name a cause that you're passionate about."

"That's easy! Anti-bullying," he announced with a smile.

"Great," said Pitts. "So, she'll go to the principal and offer to market and promote a one-on-one charity basketball game against my little sister Sandy." His mouth stretched into a vengeful smile.

"Okay," said Petey. "Cool. We'll let her know."

Peace, dweebs."

"Can you believe it? We softened his heart just a little bit," said Ruthie.

"Yeah, that might need to go in the Guinness Book of World Records," said Pudge.

The next day, in Ms. Goozerbee's class, Petey passed a note back to Penny. It read: *When you confess to Principal Strongarm, tell her that you will promote and play in a one-on-one charity basketball game supporting anti-bullying in exchange for her not telling your parents what you did.*

Penny read the note. Once Mrs. Goozerbee turned her back to write the questions to the assignment on the board, she wrote back: *Good idea. I plan to talk to her today. But who's going to be my opponent?*

Petey wrote back: *Pitts' little sister, Sandy. I already asked.*

"Thank you," whispered Penny.

Petey turned halfway around and smiled and nodded at Penny. She smiled back.

Friday morning, during music class, Petey, Ruthie, and Pudge were excited to learn to play the African drums. "This is awesome," said Pudge.

Mr. Siu was assigning each student to a drum when, suddenly, he was cut off by the public announcement system.

"Good morning, teachers and students. I apologize for the interruption. However, you'll be glad to know that the culprit responsible for the food fights in the cafeteria has confessed to the crime and will be dealt with accordingly. Therefore, during lunchtime today, I urge you to enjoy yourselves as the silent lunch ban is being lifted. I repeat, the silent lunch ban has been lifted. Please enjoy your lunch today."

"Wahoo!" screamed Petey.

Cheers of relief and excitement from all the students bounced off the thin walls throughout the school. The students in Mr. Siu's class were sooooo ecstatic that they began beating on the drums without his instruction.

At lunchtime, as the gang was standing in line to get their lunches, they spotted Penny stapling flyers to the bulletin boards outside, as well as passing them out to students. Petey walked outside to talk to her.

"Can I have a flyer, please?" he asked.

"Sure!" she said.

"So, how did it go?"

Penny placed a white flyer on the bulletin board and, with the base of her hand, hammered the stapler into the cork board.

"Well, she yelled at me and expressed how disappointed she was in me. However, she liked your idea, and she said that because I showed courage by coming forward and offered a resolution, she won't tell my parents."

"Well, ya see, it worked out.

128

"I just want to get this over with. What a disaster I've created."

"Okay, well, I guess I better get back to lunch."

"Once again, Petey, thanks," she said.

Petey reentered the cafeteria. "So, how did she take it?" asked Pudge.

"She's actually taking it pretty well."

"Who cares? She's caused more than enough drama. I can't wait for this game! Prissy Penny won't have a chance." said Charlie.

Chapter 10

For the next few days, Penny did a lot of advertising and promotion for the upcoming game. Not only did she make flyers, but she made posters and passed out custom-made stickers and pencils promoting the basketball game. By the time the big day rolled around, her levels of anxiety had hit the ceiling. Her heart was racing, and she couldn't focus on her classwork that day because she was too nervous.

Why did I listen to Petey? What if I lose? I'm not good at basketball. What will people say? What is my opponent like? All these nerve-wracking questions clouded her head. "Oh my green beans! I'm playing basketball. And I'm playing today!" she shouted as the dismissal bell rang. Suddenly, the surrounding chatter came to a halt, and puzzled eyes were momentarily glued to Penny.

She put on a bashful smile, her heart pounding, and said, "Remember, people, the charity basketball game is in two hours. Come out and support."

She rushed out of class and ran to the girls' locker room. The game would start in an hour. She paced back and forth in front of the lockers. *Just breathe*, she told herself. *Breathe*. She suddenly began using the breathing techniques she'd learned from the Lamaze class she'd gone to when her mother had been pregnant with her baby sister. "Hee hee hoo! Hee hee hoo!" Then she began looking in the mirror and dancing to her own song. "Chee burger chee burger! Booga booga booga burger! Chee burger che burger! booga booga booga burger!"

After dancing and giving herself a pep talk for over half an hour, she looked at the clock and realized that she only had fifteen minutes left. *I'll stretch and get warmed up*, she thought.

As Penny left the locker room and approached the gym, her heart began to sink into her stomach. She could hear the students chanting and Mr. Funkberry's soulful voice leading the cheers of the crowd. Mr. Funkberry chanted:

Stand up and fight

Bullying is wrong,

Don't bully bully bully in a no-bully zone!

No-bully zone!

No-bully zone!

No-bully zone!

While the students were chanting, Penny began practicing her jump shots. Suddenly, a girl about two inches shorter than her, with orange curly hair and freckles, walked onto the court. By the time she got to the middle where Mr. Funkberry stood in the middle of the court, the cheering of the crowd had come to an absolute halt. The faces in the crowd were staring at this young girl so hard because of her fit physique. The muscles in her arms were tightly curved, and her thighs were the size and shape of watermelons.

Mr. Funkberry looked in the young girl's direction. "I assume you must be the mystery opponent?"

"Yes," she replied in a squeaky, raspy voice.

"What is your name?" he asked.

As the young girl's cheeks inflated with joy, a small portion of her right cheek sank in, and her freckles became more visible. "Sandy," she said with a smile.

Eww, her cheeks look like sesame bagels, Penny thought as she smirked.

"Since it's just the two of you playing the game," said Mr. Funkberry, "we won't use the full court. It makes it easier for you guys to do yo' thang, and there are only two quarters, so you should be able to hang." He then turned toward the crowd and announced:

Supporting anti-bullying is why we're here.

I ask all of you to join in and spread the cheer.

Give it up to these two opponents that have no fear.

They're playing for a cause,

what a brave way to set the atmosphere.

On one side, we have Sandy.

On the other side, we have Penny.

Supporters of anti-bullying,

with this crowd, we have good and plenty.

So, let's get it on in this no-bully zone!

The crowd cheered as Mr. Funkberry stood in between Sandy and Penny and threw the ball up in the air. Sandy swiftly grabbed the ball and dribbled to the basket. Penny attempted to block her path, but she circled around to the left and released the ball for two points.

Penny grabbed the ball and dribbled to half-court. As she attempted to get closer to the basket, Sandy swiped the ball from her right hand, dribbled, spun around, and scored an easy layup.

Penny took the ball out again, and Sandy raced in front of her, her eyes fixated on the ball as it went back and forth between Penny's hand and the floor.

Penny could see that Sandy was looking for another turnover. She tried to dodge Sandy as she and the ball swayed right and left, right and left. Sandy added pressure, and Penny was forced to release the ball, and SMACK!! Sandy slapped the ball out of her hand, dribbled a few steps, and executed a jump shot.

Penny looked at the scoreboard with fury. "Six to zip," she scoffed.

She mustered up the beast within her and drove full force to the basket, only to fall on her face and slide under it. Utterly embarrassed, she pounded her fist and kicked the floor as mixed emotions from the crowd soared. Penny could hear plenty of laughs and giggles from the crowd, and she was sure the ridicule was from every kid that she had intimidated or bullied.

On the other hand, there were other students, like Ruthie, who were worried about her. Ruthie got up from her seat. "I'm going to go check on her," she said.

Bustah pulled her back. "Ruthendra," he said, "this is not our fight."

Torn between what Bustah had said and what she wanted to do, Ruthie surrendered and cautiously sat back down. She understood that if Bustah were calling her by her whole first name, that meant this was serious business.

While Penny's face was buried on the court from embarrassment, Sandy knelt beside her, patted her on the back, and whispered, "Fury produces failure. If you can look up, you need to get up. We have a cause to support and a game to finish." She grabbed Penny's hand and helped her up.

Ruthie yelled, "Way to go, Penny!"

The kids sitting around her stared and rolled their eyes at her as if she were crazy. *My goodness, she thought. No one in here really likes her. Boy is this a rough crowd.*

Mr. Funkberry stared at Sandy with a sparkle in his eyes. "You're out of sight, helping your opponent during her plight! With me, you're aaaalllllriiight!" he said as he threw the ball to Sandy.

The first quarter continued, and Penny struggled as Sandy blocked shot after shot. "Oh, come on!" she yelled. "This is not fair!"

Well aware that she could demolish Penny in this game, Sandy allowed her to score three baskets near the end of the first quarter. Sandy figured if she let Penny score a couple of points, Penny wouldn't be so quick to forfeit the game and they would be able to play until the end. Sandy hated forfeiting and always worked hard to finish strong and see things through no matter how exhausted she was.

By the end of the first quarter, the score was twenty-two to six, with Sandy in the lead. *What a stupid, stupid idea this was*, Penny thought. The girls were given a ten-minute break, and she plopped down on the bench with her arms folded across her chest.

"Hey, Penny!" a student yelled. "Your performance is cheap." Everyone chuckled. Penny didn't dare turn her back to confront him.

Another student yelled, "Hey, Penny, why don't you round up your attitude and game to a dollar."

"Ooooooh!" the crowd exclaimed.

Penny huffed and puffed, and her eyes began to swell as the overflow of tears erupted. Suddenly, it began to set in that she was not as popular and powerful as she'd once thought she was. She felt the wrath and the verbal and emotional torture she'd unleashed upon other students echoing back to her in that very moment.

Minutes later, Mr. Funkberry blew his whistle, signaling to the crowd that the game was back in session. "It's the last quarter, daughters! Go out and play like anti-bullying is a must! This is a no-bully zone. Trust."

Quarter two began with Penny taking the ball out and dribbling to the basket for a potential layup, only to have the ball roll around the rim and off the basket. Sandy quickly grabbed the ball and laid it up for two more points. She moved so fast Penny didn't know what happened.

For the next few plays, Penny ended up chasing Sandy around the court, struggling to get the ball. Every time the ball was in her possession, she only had it five seconds before Sandy's dominance produced another steal. At this point, there were only eight minutes left in the quarter. Penny folded her arms, stomped her feet, and crashed her bottom on the court floor. The crowd was laughing hysterically. With the clock still counting down, she was not only losing minutes, but patience as well.

Mr. Funkberry rushed over to her. "Let's go, Penny. Don't give up now. Even if you lose, the cause you're supporting is more powerful than the foul."

Sandy walked over to Penny and extended her hand. "Get up now, Penny," she demanded. "This is not about you. It's about a cause. This is so much bigger than you. We got six minutes left. Focus."

The truth of the matter was that it was about Penny and the chaos and inconvenience she'd imposed on other students because of her selfishness. She reluctantly tugged on Sandy's hand as Sandy pulled her up off the floor. She gazed at the scoreboard, which read thirty-five to six and pressed on to finish the game. Her muscles began to ache as she screamed up and down half-court to reach zero minutes in the game.

The amount of fatigue and exhaustion that she was experiencing was so overbearing that those last five minutes felt like five hours. Let's face it, she wasn't an athlete like Sandy. She wasn't trained to endure.

Sandy had nailed the last three shots, and Penny's eyes were glued to the clock. As the mustard seed of strength she had left subsided, she collapsed on the floor, and the crowd chanted, "Ten, nine, eight, seven, six, five, four, three, two, one."

"And that's the game, kiddo diddos!" announced Mr. Funkberry. Sandy rushed over to help Penny up, but she declined the offer and pleaded for Mr. Funkberry to hand her the microphone. He honored her request and patted her on the back as she spoke.

Sandy noticed Penny's legs were weak and brought her a chair. "Have a seat, "she said.

"Thank you, Penny replied. Then, to the crowd, she said, "Listen, today had to be the biggest challenge in my life. I get it now. I get it now." She nodded her head. "And I'm so sorry for anyone I've ever harmed in any type of way. Ever since my baby sister was born, I've felt that my parents forgot about me. I was so selfish and inconsiderate. I was upset that the attention was no longer all on me, and I took it out on each and every last one of you. What you felt over the last year is what I felt on this court today, and I deserve every bit of it. I was intimidated by my mystery opponent, who encouraged me throughout the game when I wanted to quit. In this short time, she trained me in the importance of endurance just like I've trained you guys about endurance but in a negative way. I'm sorry that you guys had to endure those silent lunches. And Milton, wherever you are, I'm sorry that I bullied you to help me start those food fights."

Gasps clouded the room, and the crowd looked on in total shock.

"The booing, laughter, and snide remarks that were echoed throughout the game were well deserved. You guys really hurt my feelings, and I felt like a victim, but vicious victims can't vacate problems they've caused when people refuse to vindicate them. They have to stand up and own their parts in their convictions. So, I say to you, my name is Penny Proudfoot, and at the moment, I am not proud that I was a bully."

The crowd was silent and in shock. Petey stood and began to clap. One by one, the rest of the gang rose to their feet. Pitts reluctantly joined them, clapping as well.

Penny rushed to the gym exit, embarrassed. Principal Strongarm followed her. "Penny, that was awesome, and you exhibited a great level of growth and maturity. I'm proud of you," she said as she eagerly grabbed Penny and gave her a tight hug. The warmth and comfort of Principal Strongarm's embrace allowed Penny to weep uncontrollably. Principal Strongarm stroked Penny's long blonde hair as she rocked her in her arms.

The next morning, the gang stood under the tree, chit-chatting before the first bell rang. "Penny did a very brave thing yesterday, "said Pudge.

"Yeah, mane," said Diego. "Not many people can admit their mistakes in front of a crowd like that."

Charlie fiddled with the dusty sand and green leaves on the ground. "Well, believe it or not, I'm proud of her. Ya know I neva cared for her. But she did a good deed this time. I hope this means she gon' turn ova a new leaf."

"We shall see," said Bustah and Ruthie in unison.

Chapter 11

Minutes later, the first bell rang, and the gang headed to class. Chattering and giggles echoed throughout Mr. Funkberry's class when Diego, Charlie, and Bustah entered the room.

"Settle down, kiddo diddos, while I take roll. Watch out now, don't get out of control," said Mr. Funkberry. "Aristide, Brownlee, Li, Mitchell, Peterson, Santiago, Williams…"

Suddenly, a tall boy the size of a palm tree entered the room, peering with intensity at his right hand as his fingers twitched rapidly. He wore orange headphones, a black shirt with a picture of techno artist Green Velvet, khaki shorts, and black Chucks. A weary, middle-aged woman followed him. She glanced around anxiously at the room full of spooky eyes filled with wonder staring back at her.

She spoke privately with Mr. Funkberry in the front corner of the room near his desk. Mr. Funkberry turned towards the class and announced, "Attention, class. Oh, what a treat it is to meet Cokey Michaels." Charlie leaned forward and whispered at the back of Bustah's neck, "Cokey? Does Cokey even know that we're here?"

As Bustah looked around the silent room, he noticed that the rest of the students seemed to be in a weird trance that they needed to snap out of. Sure, they'd never experienced anything like this, but he didn't want the weary lady to freak out. He shouted quickly, "Come on, Funkaroos, let's welcome Cokey!" and he clapped rapidly.

"Yayeee, Cokey!" shouted Charlie.

The rest of the class folded their hands and swayed their arms from ear to ear as they shouted, "Funk-funk-aroo! Funk-funk-aroo!"

The weary-faced lady smiled with a sigh of relief and walked Cokey to the empty seat in front of Bustah. As she moved in to give him a peck on the cheek, he mushed her face with his left hand and yelled, "Stop it, Mom!" Feeling slightly embarrassed, his mom exited the room.

Cokey continued twitching his fingers for the majority of the class period. It seemed as if he were totally ignoring Mr. Funkberry.

Midway through class, Charlie walked to the front of the room to sharpen her pencil. Cokey was immediately drawn to her orange curly hair. As she turned around to go back to her desk, with no facial expression, he said, "You look like a Cheeto."

Chuckles and giggles filled the room. Charlie leaned in closer to Cokey. "Oh, you—"

Bustah yelled, "No!" and shook his head at Charlie. She figured he had a good reason as to why he wouldn't let her give Mr. Cokey a piece of her mind. She gave him an evil stare as she plopped down in her seat.

Bustah stared at the back of Cokey Michael's head with intense curiosity. *There's something about Cokey Michaels. We've got to get to the bottom of this*, he thought.

Curious to know more about Cokey Michaels? Well, check out the second book in this series: *There's Something about Cokey Michaels.*

About the Author

T.T. Floyd was born in Miami, Florida. As a child, her fifth-grade teacher Mrs. Willie Mae McClain inspired her love for writing and encouraged her to enter in writing and poetry contests. While most of her friends were thrilled to go outside to play, T.T. preferred to stay in the house reading, writing, as well as creating and performing in her own soap opera. Her love for writing continued to flourish throughout high school. In high school she was a staff writer and feature editor for her school newspaper, The *Smoke Signal*. "What excites me most about writing is when the characters that I create take me on an unpredictable journey." T.T. Floyd is a three-time graduate of Nova Southeastern University. She resides in Pembroke Pines, FL with her loving husband David Floyd and their three children David Jr., Taylor, and Dylan.

Made in the USA
San Bernardino, CA
03 June 2020